Kurbaan

Flairs and Glairs

Publication House

"Kurbaan"

ISBN No: " 9789391302092"
1st Edition
Language – English and Hindi

Flairs and Glairs
Publication House
Regd. Under MSME Act.

Copyright. 2021, Sahina Ghugha

All Rights are Reserved. No Part of this can be reproduced, stored, copied or transmitted in any form may it be electronic, mechanical, magnetic, optical, photocopies, and or any other possible manner without the prior written approval of the author and publication house, except for a reference in respect to the author or the publishing entity work.

Disclaimer

This is a work of fiction and solely represent the thoughts of the corresponding authors of the articles. Our editors have tried their best to edit the content of all the authors and check the plagiarism.

All the write-ups in this book are unique and are only published in this book.

In case a ny plagiarism or error is found, only the author is responsible alone, and not the publisher or the Compilers.

Cover Designing and Book Formatting
Shubham Shah and Ishani Agarwal

Acknowledgment

My primary thanks to God. I am blessed with the energy to be able to complete this anthology.
I also thankful towards our whole team of "Flairs and Glairs Publication".

I am thankful to my parents, Mr. Salim Ghugha and Mrs. Reshma Ghugha for trusting and supporting me always. And my friends and extended family to support in every step of life. And to provide me a surrounding where I can raise my voice for all types of issues.

Thank you all the co-authors, without your support we would never be able to complete this anthology.

Co Author

Shubham Shah (Founder Flairs and Glairs)
Ishani Agarwal (Co-Founder Flairs and Glairs)
Muskan Shah (Project Head)
Sahina Ghugha (Compiler)

1. Kavitha Subramani
2. Jagriti Pramanik
3. Md Monif Akhtar
4. Shaheen Banu
5. Kiran Tiwari
6. Neha Gupta
7. Dia Dey
8. Poonam Naik
9. Gaurangi Mishra
10. Garvita Mishra
11. Saumya Agrawal
12. Prakriti Garg
13. Sonia Chhabra
14. Rajeshwari Chaubey
15. Abhinaya Reddy
16. Mehtaz Nasrin Ahmed
17. Ritu Sachdeva
18. Divya Nokhwal
19. Sureka Velusamy
20. Punam Nikalje

Shubham Shah

(Founder- Flairs and Glairs)

Shubham Shah, an entrepreneur at "Flairs & Glairs" a brand with dynamics in events organizing and cultural educational pan INDIA, is a 26yrs old guy who recently has entered the digital platform of imprinting emotions. He has initiated with his own open mic platform to help budding poets and aspiring writers under his brand named as "Teekhe Zasbaaat"

He is a commerce graduate from the Bhagalpur City of Bihar. He states Writing has impersonated him since childhood and he has now been writing for over a decade!

Cooking, on the other hand, is his passion! He also mentions, trying out new things just tickles him!

When asked sir, Why SPICY EMOTIONS?

He smiled and added, "agar jasbaat teekhe na ho toh wo jasbaat kahan" Spices are all that blends! So do his words!

As a chef, he presents to you his dish! Hot and freshly served! Taste it! Feel it! Enjoy it! You can also find his writing in the Book "Teekhe Zasbaaat" and 50+ Co -authored anthologies.

With his passion to explore opportunities across Platforms, he is working with keen devotion and We wish him all the very best for his future ventures.

He is Featured in the International Magazine DeMode for his upcoming solo novel.

He is Approved by Ne8x for its Lit Fest, and is a Golden Star Awards 2020 Winner.

He is a India Book of Records Holder for his Anthology Satrang, and has the Grandmaster title by Asia Book of Records, for the same.

He has also been featured in Prabhat Khabar, Dainik Jagran, and a lot of other Newspapers in Bihar for his achievements.

He has been a proud co-author to

India Book Of Records (Title- Black)

World Book Of Records (Title -15 Wonders of Poetries)

India Book Of Records (Title - Aaina)

Vajra World Records Holder (Title - Gustakhi Maaf Hai)

High Range of Records Holder (Title - Gustakhi Maaf Hai)

Indian Book of Records

(Title - Road from Worst to Best)

Share your reviews on his

INSTAGRAM

@spicy_emotions
@shubham4shah

Or via email on

shubham2shah@gmail.com

To stay tuned to his work and opportunities follow his business
Handles

INSTAGRAM   FACEBOOK   YOUTUBE

@flairsandglairs
@teekhezasbaaat

WEBSITE:

https://flairsandglairs.in/
https://flairsandglairs.com/

Ishani Agarwal

(Co-Founder- Flairs and Glairs)

Ishani Agarwal hails from the City of Joy, Kolkata.
She is the co -founder of her Community "Teekhe Zasbaaat"
and Flairs and Glairs Publication.
Been a Compiler for 45+ Anthologies, she is in the process for
more. Co-authored in 150+ Anthologies. She is a India Book
of Records Holder, a   Vajra World Records Holder, a High
Range of Records Holder, an OMG Book of Records Holder,
a Bravo Record holder, a Forever Star Book of World Records
and an Indian Book of Records Holder.
Approved by Ne8x for its Lit Fest 2020, and Literary Icon
2020. Also a Golden Star Awards Winner 2020.
She has also been awarded with India Star Republic Award
2021, a part of She Awards by Awards Arc and Winner of Nari
Samman 2021 by Literoma.

She is also selected as Best Achiever of the Year by AwardsArc and Most Challenging Compiler Award by Spectrum Awards.
She got her first solo Published,a solo Compilation consisting of first 750 contents of hers, titled "Hand That Burnt While Healing".

She has been featured by the National Magazine "Taree Zameen Par" with the title 'unstoppable'.
Also featured in the International Magazine DeMode for her upcoming solo novel, she is proud to write on social issues, and is happy with the love she is receiving.
Connect with her on Instagram: @Ishani_agarwal_quotes / @compilations_so_far

Muskan Shah
(Project Head)

Muskan Shah hails from Jharsuguda, Odisha. She is a Company Secretary Professional Student. She has completed her Interior Designing from Arena Animations, Bilaspur. She is a growing Poetess and has performed in various poetry events.

Sahina Ghugha
(Compiler)

Sahina Ghugha is 20 year old B.com student at Saurashtra university Rajkot. She is from Jamnagar city of Gujarat. She is Co-author in 50+ anthologies. She compiled 3 anthologies named "Hoax feelings", "Joker" and "Murad   - Ek Ummid". She is an amazing writer and poet and she wants do something for society through her pen.

Insta ID:-
Itz_Sahina_writes

Kavitha Subramani

Kavitha Subramani is 22 year old   doing M.A. English Language and Literature. She is from Erode city of Tamil Nadu. She is a co-author of 7+ anthologies. She is an amazing writer and poet. She wants do something effective through her pen.

Wondered

I wondered
When I saw the trees
I admired by the leaves and branches
How it's seperate oxygen from air
And how it's sacrifice?
I admired by the way of flowing.

I wondered
When the fresh air touch the sky
Clouds became dark
Chillness spread the world
Before the arrival of drops
Everyone feel the climatic change
When it touch the earth
Excitement filled with joy
Each drops offering life for the world.

I wondered
When I saw the water
Paved way for join together
I admired when it
Provoke the grass to grow
When it grows well
Offered itself as a food.

I wondered
When I saw the soliders
They loss their
Entire life for our nation
Families are forgotten
Happiness are gifted
Souls and bloods are surrender
For the welfare of our country

Lots of pains came across
Lots of sleepless nights
To be remembered
Lots of tears fall down
Whatever happened, they accept it
But they offer peace, secure
And happy life for us.

I wondered
When I saw my mother
How she controls her pain?
I know that before my birth
I make her to suffer a lot
But, when she saw my face
Her pain vanished
She offering her wishes
For my happiness
Each and everything done
For my goodness
Even bare her physical pain
For my joy
Unforgettable torches
To be remembered
But her sacrifice towards me
Never return back.

I wondered
When I saw my father
He is the one who lead
His entire life for my comfort.
Still, I remembered the day
When he skip his food for me
Most of the time
He made my stomach filled with food
But his stomach filled with water

He provides well dresses for me
But he never mind about his own
If I do mistakes
He rectified me
If I do good
He stands as a pillar behind me
His each steps
Contains multi- losses, but
It's only for me.

Every surrender contains
A new beginning
Behind every sacrifice
Pure soul is hidden
The entire world filled with
Lots of gifts and losses.

Jagriti Pramanik

Jagriti Pramanik hails from Odisha and is a teacher by profession. She believes in miracles and welcomes them with open arms. She finds peace in reading and spending time with nature in any form.

Silhouette Of His Inspiration- His Father

He held my hand during my first steps of life,
He gave me the best piggy back rides ever,
He walked those thousand miles to fulfill my wish of 'my first cycle'.
He became my candle during my late night studies,
He skipped his meals to afford my admission in the best institute,
He did overtime to educate me without any financial hassle,
He dropped out from his schooling to fulfill my dreams.

He sacrificed his family life to construct my career,
He walked with me in every step of my life,
He was a shield to me all these years.
I was focused in my studies because he was my inspiration,
I touched the apex of accomplishment because he was my pillar,
I got recognition because he cultured me into a crystal,
I have a life of comfort because he gave up his opportunities,
I reached the heights of success because he let me mount his shoulders.

I wasn't privileged to see my father during my birth,
'Coz before my arrival he left the earth,
But I proudly can say that I never missed my dad,
Because I have my 'BROTHER' not less than my father.
Had my father been alive, he would be like my brother,
My brother is the most precious treasure of my life,
Yes, he is indeed the 'Silhouette' of his inspiration-my father.

Secret Love…

She treasured him with all her sentiment and passion,
He admired her with all his seriousness,
Their love was uncontaminated, cherished, and concrete.
They tried to hide their love from the world,
But like a force of lava that oozes out of a consequence of
heat inside,
Their love too stormed radiating its glory to a new level of
intimacy.

They shared their moments with each other being distant,
The distance was not intended or shaped by them,
Their affection couldn't be concealed.
Their eyes mirrored care and support for each other,
Nobody was against their unity,
But there was still something that kept them detached.

Everything was organized yet nothing was thorough,
Things were organized yet nothing was carried out,
To unite them into a nuptial relation,
I still wonder what is going wrong.
Is it their insecure commitment to one another?
Or is it their mutual sacrifice behind their fear of acceptance
by society?

They can't stand the separation from one another even for
days,
But uniting in a thread of happiness was as if not the plan of
fortune,
But the strings they are knotted are magically resilient and
strong.

I Am Sorry I Couldn't Witness

I am sorry I couldn't witness the star in you
With a blink of an eye time changed,
The perennial flow of the streams blocked,
The tweeting of the birds hushed,
The tints of the environment faded off,
The blossoming flowers shed off,
Why was everything so still and solitary?

Because there was no one to embrace them,
He thought while gazing at the gleaming stars,
As if penetrating her in the intensity of hours of darkness.

The night dozed off for weeping late,
Nobody now turned over his plate,
His phone did not blaze any missed call,
But he could only see her confined in a photo frame on the
wall,
Nobody waits for him on dinner,
He keeps blaming himself for being a sinner.

Months passed away in her memories,
But to survive he could not find a way,
They were united in a relation of friends since childhood,
But were they really lovers?
He was accustomed of her that he couldn't go without,
He was her friend he couldn't find a way.
They were coupled into many relations in this one life,
But failed to play the role of husband and wife,
She was insubstantial he was naïve,
She was accountable he was generous.

But what went mistaken, was their perfection,

She understood his melancholy,
He kept taking her for granted,
He was contented with her,
But was she at bliss with him?
Her sacrifice opened his eyes,
When he lost her in his heart's skies.
Yes, by sacrificing her life,
She made him a fine being of maturity and understanding.

But he did not comprehend her charisma,
Until he came across her absence,
Love lived in them connecting them insanely,
But the passion faded away steadily,
And now he is in a state of lonesome,
Spending days and nights in her sweet reminiscence,
But she had to sacrifice her life to investigate his inner self,
While converting into a star too she gave her radiance to him.

Quotes

1. There's nothing wrong if a woman thinks about her happiness
There is nothing rude if a woman voices out her opinions
She is a warrior in every sense.
Right from her birth till her death
She has been in a race to chisel her
And emerging into an indomitable soul
So, there's nothing weird,
If they choose diamonds as their best friends
Coz like a diamond they are unique,
Elegant and dangerous too.
Yes, that's what a WOMAN is.

2. Your absence makes my life void of happiness and peace.
But it's also true that I found my presence in my life in your absence.

3. The heart finds its peace not in rage but in prayers that mention the well -being of that one person who might be the person responsible for this emptiness.

4. She was very talkative once,
Because there were people who heard her without any percipience
 She was so naïve to have numerous friends,
But with time, things changed so quickly.
She still has lots of friends,
But she is too lonesome to share her agony with even one
 She is occupied still void of company.

Md Monif Akhtar

Md Monif Akhtar from Bihar is good at write poems and qoutes, he is Co-author of 2 books. His writings are published in the book named "Hoax Feeling's" .

पुकार

माँ
मैं जनता हूं कि
तुम बहुत परेशान हो
मेरे लिए चिंतित हो
मुझे पता है तुमने अपनी खाना भी नहीं खाया।।
माँ
लेकिन जब में यहां आया था
तो हम सबको पता था
मेरा कोई तो कल है ही नहीं
फिर क्यों रोती हो मां।।
माँ
तू मेरी हिम्मत है
अगर तू ही टूट गई तो
मैं कैसे सरहद पर खड़ा रह सकता हूं ?
माँ
मुझे माफ़ करना
आज धरती मईया के सामने
तेरी ममता पीछे रह गई ।।
माँ
रो मत ऐसे तू
मैं सो नहीं पा रहा हूं
मां छोटी बहन को बोल
उसके और भाई अभी सरहद पर खड़े हैं
पापा को समझा, मरा नहीं हूं शहीद हूं
मैं तो अमर हूं
फिर क्यों ऐसे रोते हो ?
माँ
मैं जहां हूं बहुत खुश हूं

तू ही तो कहा करती थी
फर्ज पहले है फिर हम है
क्यों फिर ऐसे बिलखती है ?
माँ
देख ज़रा मेरे लाल को
इसे ये ही तुझे समझाना है
बाप इसका मरा नहीं
बस शहीद हुआ है
अकेला नहीं हूं यहां
तुम सबकी यादें है।।
माँ
मेरी संगनी को समझा
विधवा नहीं है वो
वो, वो औरत है जिसने अपना
सर्वांग न्योछावर किया है, इस मिट्टी पर
उसे तो अभी एक ओर
जवान तैयार करना है
मेरा लाल मुझसे भी बड़ा योद्धा बनेगा।।
माँ
अब बस बहुत हुआ
एक काम तू भी कर
एक फुलवाड़ी लगा
और उन पौधों को
पाल ऐसे जैसा तेरा लाल हो
फिर वो भी अपनी छवि से
एक दिन तेरा नाम रोशन कर
दुनिया में अमन चैन लाएंगे।।
माँ
अब दे विदा तू मुझे
चैन से अब मैं सोऊंगा

बोल दे उन गद्दारो को
जिसने मेरी मिट्टी पर बुरी नजर डाली
चैन उनका छीन लूँगा
अब दे विदा मुझे

ये धरती मेरी धड़कन है
ये धरती मेरी जान है।
चलो एक दिन ही सही पर याद करे उन लोगो को जिनके लहु के
अब भी निशान है

आज़ादी

हर रोज उस सिमा पर आजादी के लिए लडते अब भी जवान है।
इस केसरिया तिरंगे झंडे पर देखो कितने लोग कुर्बान है
चलो याद करे उनकी कुर्बानी को
चलो याद करे जिन्होंने खोई अपनी जवानी को
जो सहा हमारे अपनो ने उन पर बीती उन बात पुरानी को
कुछ पल ही सही कुछ क्षण ही सही बस याद करो उनकी कहानी को
टुट पड़े वो सौ पर एक
पर सिर पर नाम हिन्दुस्तान था
मौत को गले लगाया
मुख पर लेकर मुस्कान था
वो रूके नहीं वो थके नहीं उनके ऊपर भरा इस चोले का जुनून था
जिस पानी से इस धरती ने नहाया वो क्रांतिकारीयो का खून था
जो देश के लिए मर मिटे उनके लिए ये कविता सम्मान है
चलो एक दिन ही सही पर याद करे उन लोगों को जिनके लहू के अब भी निशान हैं।

वह कौन है?

मिट्टी वतन की पूछती वह कौन है, वह कौन है?
इतिहास जिस पर मौन है?

जिसके लहू की बूंद का टीका हमारे भाल पर,
जिसके लहू की लालिमा स्वातंत्र शिशु के गाल पर,
जो बुझ गया गिर कर गगन से, निमिष में तारा–सदृश,
बच ओस जितना भी न पाया, अश्रु जिसका काल पर

जो दे गया जीवन विजन के फूल सा हँस नाश को...
जिसके लिये दो बूंद भी स्याही नहीं इतिहास को?
वह कौन है, वह कौन है?

जिसके मरण के नेह से, दीपक नये युग का जला,
काजल नयन के मेह से, मरुथल मनुज–मन का फला,
चुनता गया पद–पद्य से, कंटक मनुज की राह का,
विष दासता को, मुक्ति को, निज मृत्यु का अमृत पिला,
चुभती न स्मृति जिसकी कभी, जो मैं किसी के शूल–सी,
झरते न जिस पर आंख से, दो आंसुओं के फूल ही!

Shaheen Banu

She is shaheen, her friend would describe her as good listener, good counsler and good writer also once "a writing teacher told her that the most successful movies and books were smiple
Plots about complex characters .....you should be able to articulate your concept in a couple of lines.

Success

"Sucess Is no accident it is hard work preseverance, learning, studying, SACRIFICE,and most of all love of what you are doing or learning to do What is sacrifice.....?Sacrifice means ignoring many desirable personal goals in the pursuit of one or relatively few other goals such as extreme wealth and/or professional success. Altruists are no t the only ones making personal sacrifices to achieve their primary goal(s). Many leaders and celebrities sacrifice family, close friendships, and relatively mundane pleasures for leadership or celebrity success. Working hard to acquire new skills and know   ledge seems like sacrificing a life of leisure and indulgence for many but to the hard workers it is means opening up new possibilities for future beneficial opportunities. If you are not ignoring important things then you are not sacrificing them and if y ou are ignoring trivial things then sacrificing them is almost an obligation.I will start with very great example of Parents.

They have done so many sacrifices for us most of these we don't even notice. They sacrifice their entire life,dream,career just to make sure we are happy. They don't buy new stuff to make sure we get latest phone.new bike ,brand new clothes etc etc .. there is no limit of sacrifices they have done so far and they will do in coming days selflessly. So, Coming back to your question what is Sacrifice "It is act when one left/forget his own profit/passion/career/wish to make sure or full -fill other's happiness" and as I already mentioned Our parents , our Family is best example.

Story

This question remind me a story of A King and A Sa ge , that tells about the real meaning of Sacrifice : Once there was a king who was always fighting. One day he was badly wounded in a battle. A sage passed by and touched him, and the king was cured. He wanted to give the sage a reward for saving him, but the sage didn't want anything.

The king said, "I don't want to be indebted to you." The sage said, "In the future I'll ask for something. I don't need anything now, but one day I'll come." Months passed and the sage was praying to God one day for peace,   light and bliss, when a desire entered his mind. For the past few months his cow had not been producing milk. "She's old," he said. "I'll ask the king for a new cow." He went to see the king and found him in a temple. He was praying for more wealth and mor   e fame. The sage said to himself, "I won't ask him for a cow. He's a beggar like me." And he turned to leave. The king stopped him and said, "Sage, you saved my life. Please tell me what you want. I'll give you anything." The sage said, "I pray to God and meditate. He is all I need. I don't want to take anything from anyone in need. You told me you took an oath that you would not be indebted to anyone. I, too, have taken an oath. My oath is that if anyone is in need, then I won't take anything from that person.

That's why I won't take anything from you. You're praying to God for material things. You're begging for God to give you wealth and fame. So how can I ask anything of you? God has shown me that everyone is a beggar. So if I need something, I'll get i t from Him."What is sacrifice? AI & Machine Learning course for working professionals. This question remind me a story of A King and A Sage , that tells about the

real meaning of Sacrifice : Once there was a king who was always fighting. One day he was badly wounded in a battle. A sage passed by and touched him, and the king was cured. He wanted to give the sage a reward for saving him, but the sage didn't want anything. The king said, "I don't want to be indebted to you." The sage said, "In the future I'll   ask for something. I don't need anything now, but one day I'll come." Months passed and the sage was praying to God one day for peace, light and bliss, when a desire entered his mpain.

For the past few months his cow had not been producing milk. "She's old," he said. "I'll ask the king for a new cow." He went to see the king and found him in a temple. He was praying for more wealth and more fame. The sage said to himself, "I won't ask him for a cow. He's a beggar like me." And he turned to leave. The king stopped him and said, "Sage, you saved my life. Please tell me what you want. I'll give you anything." The sage said, "I pray to God and meditate. He is all I need. I don't want to take anything from anyone in need. You told me you took an oath that you would not be indebted to anyone. I, too, have taken an oath. My oath is that if anyone is in need, then I won't take anything from that person. That's why I won't take anything from you. You're praying to God for material things. You're begging for God to give you wealth and fame. So how can I ask anything of you? God has shown me that everyone is a beggar. So if I need something, I'll get it from Him." Life is pain.

Life is pain and suffering sporadically broken up with brief moments of pleasure. Some folks resist accepting that as true, but as has been said before: resistance if futile. :) Even too much seeking of pleasure seems to bring pain and suffering. Once we see that existance and progress/prosperity (growth) is based on facing pain and suffering (even seeking it as many sports participants know and do), then we start to see the need

for deliberate sacrifice. In fact, we could hypothesize that all significant progress came from people who decide to sacrifice to seek it and many ended up helping to a chieve it. Yes, we have a "ease seeking" gene is seems (but my guess is that it's taught as an expectation, and is not genetic). So sacrifice is seeing a path to ease/pleasure and deciding not to take that path but rather, turn away from that and choose pa in and suffering to achieve a far greater reward (for yourself, for others, in your present life, and/or for future generations, etc.).

If we look back in history, we can clearly see that we now benefit from hundreds, thousands, millions of people's pain and suffering before us. Yet we sit typing on a keyboard or reading a computer screen in safety today. A lot of unearned benefits have come our way. Many of benefits came through sacrifice and we are reaping the rewards of that. Will we continue to sacrifice for the future or will we be unappreciative and lazily think we can "coast and complain" without contributing/sacrificing like those millions did before us?
The real meaning of sacrifice in life is the "peace during dying". It means when we going to die then we have no incomplete wish or other queries. At that time we should be happy about our journy of life.

True Meaning Of Sacrifice

The true meaning of sacrifice is the giving, or giving up, of something a person considers essential to their own wellbeing, or which is of such great value that they would never consider giving it up or giving it away if the reason for giving it wasn't worth more to them than the thing itself. Technically, the idea of sacrifice is neutral about the worthiness of the reason for it. People sacrifice things in vain, or unwisely. Sacrifice is not automatically virtuous. Again, it can be done unwisely, or for the wrong motives.THE IMPORTANCE OF SACRIFICE. Success is connected to doing things that are not fun for the moment. It is connected to channeling your energy into completing that task that gives you agony and lack of enjoyment. Success equals sacrifice.Wh ile it may very well happen in this manner, one may be able to benefit in ways such as the blessings of good health – eliminating costly medical bills, protection from costly mistakes, opportunities for progress and development, gifts in kind, socializing and networking in the right crowd – those who mean you well.

the real meaning of sacrifice in life is the "peace during dying". it means when we going to die then we have no incomplete wish or other queries. at that time we should be happy about our journy of life.

Kiran Tiwari

Kiran. R. Tiwari is 24 year olddoing MBA from ROFEL vapi.
She is from valsad city of Gujarat. She is co   -author of 4+
anthologies. She is a beautiful writer. She want to be a great
writer in future

जीवन बलिदान का दूसरा नाम

जीवन बलिदान का दूसरा नाम है हर वक़्त ज़िंदगी की राहो मे उलझने, तकलीफे आती रहती हैं। मेरा मनना है की हमारी ज़िंदगी के हर मोड पर अगर किसी ने सबसे ज्यादा बलिदान दिया है तो वो है हमारे माता- पिता, जी है ! जब घर मे एक बच्चा जन्म लेता है तो उसके साथ जन्म लेती है दो हस्तियां जिन्हे हम माता- पिता कहते हैं। और फिर हमारे प्रति ज़िम्मेदारी जिन्हे वो पूरी निष्ठा से पुरा करना चाहते है और जिसके लिए न जाने वो कितना कुछ कुर्बान कर देते है।

माँ चाहती हैं की वो अपने बच्चे को ऐसे संस्कार दे, ऐसी परवरिश दे जिससे उसे भविष्य मे कभी कोई तकलीफ न आये, कोई उसके बच्चे पर उंगली न उठा सके और पिता ये चाहते है की मै मेरे बच्चे को दुनिया की वो सारी खुशी दे दु जिससे उसे कभी दुःख क्या होता है ये पता ही न चले। खुद रो कर भी हमे हसना सिखाया है, ज़िंदगी जीना भूल जाते हैं हमे जीना सिखाते-सिखाते । हर वक़्त दुनिया की बुरी नजरो से हमे बचाने की कोशीश करते है, हर वक़्त साया बन कर साथ चलते हैं, हमारे बिना कुछ कहे सब कुछ समझ जाते है, आँसू खुशी के है या गम के ये भी सिर्फ चेहरा देख कर पहचान जाते है।

मां बाप

हमारे लिए तो १२ महीने, ३६५ दिन, २४ घंटे होते है उनके लिए तो सब दिन एक समान होते है। हम तो हर मौसम को मेहसूस करते है, हमारी वजह से उन्हे पता ही नही चलता कौन सा मौसम आया और कौन सा गया। दिन रात एक कर देते है ताकि हमे अच्छी परवरिश मिल सके, अपने सपने पुरा नही कर पाते ताकि हमारे सपने पूरे हो सके। क्या कहु मै मेरे लिए तो मेरे माता पिता दोनों ही पूजनीय है, हम चार भाई बहनो को कभी किसी चीज की कमी नही होने दी, मांगने की कभी जरूरत ही नही हुई, बिना मांगे सब कुछ मिल जाता था।

माता पिता

भगवान हर जगह नही पहुँच सकते इसलिए उन्होंने हर बच्चे को माता पिता से नवाजा है। खुशनसीब है वो बच्चे जो अपनी माता पिता के साये मे पलते है। सारी सारी रात जागते जब हम बीमार होते है, परीक्षा हमारी होती है और नींद उन्हे नही आती, अपने सारे दर्द भूल जाते है हमारी एक मुस्कान देख कर। हम अपने अंग का कतरा कतरा भी बेच दे तो भी इनके बलिदान का एक हिस्सा भी नही पुरा कर सकते है। एक बात मेरे समझ नही आती कोई अपने माँ- बाप की आँखों मे आँसू कैसे दे सकते हैं। जिस उम्र मे उनके साथ होना चाहिए उस उम्र मे हम उन्हे दर दर भटकने के लिए छोड सकते है। जो बचपन मे हमारा सहारा बनते थे, जिनकी उंगली पकड़ कर चलना सीखे थे, गीर जाते थे तो गोद मे उठा लेते

त्याग

जिन्होंने हमारे लिए अपना सब कुछ त्याग दीया ये सोच कर की ये बच्चे हमारे बुढ़ापे का सहारा बनेंगे और यहाँ सहारा तो दूर की बात उनके पास बैठने तक का वक़्त नही है। मुझे समझ नही आता कुछ लोग इतनी हिम्मत कहा से लाते है की अपने माँ -बाप से ये बोल सके की आप हमे समझते ही नही हो, या नही समझोगे, और कुछ की हद तो तब होती है जब ये पूछे की आप लोगो ने हमारे लिए किया ही क्या है। हम ये क्यों नही सोचते की जब हम बोल भी नही पाते थे तब हमारी तोतली भाषा भी वो समझ जाते थे और आज जब बोलने लगे है ,जिनकी वजह से हम अपने पैरो पर खड़े हो सकते है, तो तुमने सोच कैसे लिया की वो तुम्हे नही समझेंगे या वो तुम्हे समझते नही है। हमारे लिए पूरी दुनिया कदमो मे रख दी और हम पूछते है की हमारे लिए किया ही क्या है, माफ करना इस दुनिया मे अगर आप कहीं सुरक्षित है तो वो सिर्फ अपने माता पिता की छाया में, यकीन मानिए अंधेरे मे आपकी परछाई तक आपका साथ छोड़ देती है, लेकिन माँ बाप का साया! उनका साया कभी भी आपका साथ नही छोड़ता।

Neha Gupta

Neha gupta was born on September 22, 1993 . She did her B.com from Satyawati college, University of Delhi. She did M.com From Indira Gandhi National Open University. She is currently pursuing Bachelor of Education from PMC college, GGSIPU. She is working as Teacher,   Co-author and social media influencer. She has created her own Instagram page named itz_neha_writes. She travelled around the world and experienced sacrifices made by women in Society . She shared some interested stories in Anthology 'Kurbaan'.

An Assassination Of Girl's Dream

This was the story of girl Miss. Drucilla. She belongs to a poor family. She wants to become An Astronaut after completing her schooling. Her father Mr. Faneesh believes that girls' responsibility
is to look for her husband, her family and children. Girls should do household chores. She was a talented and dedicated girl. She scored 94% in her board exams through Science stream. Furthermore, she gave outstanding performance in Co curricular activities in school days. Due to her Orthodox parents, she was never able to pursue her dreams. She burst into tears and begged in front of her parents to allow her to pursue her career. But, they never allowed her to become An Astronaut. After completing her schooling, Drucilla was forced to marry Mr. Jacob. Her husband Mr. Jacob used to threatened her physically, mentally, emotionally, sexually. Mr. Drucilla become victim of Domestic violence, She couldn't do anything against them because she was taught to adjust with her husband whatever he is. Drucilla faced a lot of physical injuries and psychological problems. She lost her career, goals, ambition, dreams due to superstitious beliefs and myths exist in the society. Later, she ended her life.

Dowry – A Crime

It is a story of girl Marisha. After graduation, Her father Mr. Daanish start looking for bridegroom for her daughter. Daanish runs a small cold drink and snacks shop. His earnings are too meager. He met to the person Mr. Fiyaz who has son named Advik. Daanish offered Fiyaz her daughte r for advik. When Advik met Marisha, He accepted the proposal of Daanish as Marisha is beautiful, religious and educated. Daanish is worried about marriage expenses. Daanish asked Fiyaz about his marriage expectation related to financial expenses. Fiyaz to ld to have Gold jewels, Hyundai car and Cash worth ₹ 20 lakh. Daanish felt heartless. Hethought ' How did he manage huge expenses?'. If he sold his shop, He will get around ₹2 lakh. How did he manage the rest of the expenses? He asked for the loan from ba nk, but Bank refused because he has no security to offer. He asked for the help from relatives and friends but No one is ready to listen to him. They show no sympathy and kindness. He came back home and counted her savings. It was around worth ₹ 50,000. Wh en he asked Fiyaz to reduce her dowry demand. Fiyaz said ' If you don't have money, you should not dream of marrying your daughter'. You should ask a street seller to marry her. He will be ready to accept your daughter without having financial expenses. Else, You can also give your daughter to some beggar. When Daanish heard this, He breaks down and suffered a heart attack. Her   daughter Marisha took him to hospital, but he died before reach to the hospital.

Lara – A Victim Of Violence

Mrs. Lara was a girl. She did Aeronautical Engineering. In the age of 26, Lara married to Mr. Yakshit. She was living a happy married life for two years. After that, Lara got pregnant and forced to quit her career and job. She was told to serve her husband, children and laws. The laws of Lara want to have baby boy. They refused to have a girl child because they consider her as financial burden. They want to have boy because he served the financial needs of the family, earn livelihood, supporter of old age parents. Her mother-in-law did a lot of rituals to have the boy. Lara gave birth to girl child who named Akshyra. Her laws abuse and threatened her physically and mentally to gave birth to girl child. Lara knows that it was not her mistake and tried to make her laws understand the reality. But, her laws are superstitious, Orthodox and stereotype. Her laws warned her to give birth to a boy next time. When she got pregnant, again, she gave birth to a girl child. Her laws killed that little baby girl who even didn't see this world. Her husband Yakshit gave her divorced. She felt depressed after divorce. She felt ashamed when she met to the people. She felt that she sacrificed her identity, family, career and goals for her husband and laws but didn't get anything in return. She died due to mental illness at the age of 30.

Alisha — An Angel

Alisha, a girl who born in Gujarat. She was passionate to become a Singer. Alisha participated in various singing competition during her school days. When she decided to make a career in singing, She faced a lot of criticism from parents, neighbour, relatives and peer group. They refused her to sing. She decided to run away from that place. She sacrificed her family, food, shelter to become the best singer of the world. She st ayed hungry for many days. Sometimes, She slept on the footpath. She started singing on streets. After a few months, She got an offer to sing in a café. She accepted that offer to chase her dream. Later, She met to a person in Café who gave her an opportunity to sing on her channel Sony TV. After 4 years, she got an offer to create her own music album. Today, She has created 924 music albums. She performed in 672 Shows. She also made her contribution in film industry. She is world-class singer nowadays

Wreck Of Genius Mind

It was a tale of a little girl
Who have no perception about
this ruthless world
When she emerged on the planet

She is coerced to cook food
With her little hands
When she is supposed to play with toys
She is artist of her own world
But no one let her knack to pull out

She loves to doodle on what she get
But she no way fetch book to interpret
She impelled to the field for cultivation
But never sent to school for studying

As she grown up
She is contrive to marry a man
With whom she has no bond
She is aching from heart
But persist to be tranquil

Her nucleus is smashed
But can't exhibit reflexion of that
As she was a girl
And conjecture to tweak with old folks

She is a dupe of harassment
But no one show her condolence
And put heal to her wounds
That is wreaked on her whole body

Dia Dey

Dia Dey is 18 years old BA.HONS hindi student of Delhi University.she is from new delhi . She is a good author and poet . she wants to make her future bright with her mesmerizing writeups.

मुस्कुरा कर रोते हो

अगर इतना ही गम है तो बाकियों से क्यूं नहीं कहते हो,
शायद इसलिए कि कोई जान न ले कि क्या खोया है तुमने अभी अभी
अगर इतना ही डर है तो वापस उसे मना क्यूं नहीं लेते हो
कॉफी का शौक अब रहा नही तुम्हारा
अगर इतने ही इरादों के पक्के हो तो जिंदगी एक बार फिर शुरू क्यूं
नहीं कर लेते हो।
यूं ही अक्सर बातों के बीच में से उठकर चले जाया करते हो
अगर इतने ही नाराज़ हो तो अपनी मां को एक फोन कॉल क्यूं नहीं
कर लेते हो
रो न दे वो जानकर दुख तुम्हारा शायद इसलिए तो तुम रातों में अकेले
आँसू बहाया करते हो ।

मन.....

रिमझिम रिमझिम बीता रही सफर कि यह रैना है,
अब तो सावन घट गया केवल नज़र का यह फेरा है,
मेरा मन अंत नहीं अनंत को जाता है
पुरानी यादों , बातों से यह डगमगा रहा सवेरा है
अब तो शान्त भी काफी है ओस की बूंदें वह मूंदती निगाहों से मूझपर
न्यौछावर हैं।

फ़ाक़ा मस्ती...

मै यह भी कुछ ज़हमत से कम नहीं ,
मज़ीरत में मुझसे अक्सर मिल जाती है ,
वजाहत भले न बदलती मगर फ़ाक़ामस्ती सिखाती है।

कुछ लफ्ज़....

कुछ लफ्ज़ मैं आज कुछ इस तरह लिखती हूँ
मेरी बातों को जब सहारा तुम्हारे दिल का मिला ,
तब हर वक़्त मुश्किल का थम सा गया,
मैं जानती हूं कि तुम मुझे सदा से मानते हो ,
शायद इसलिए मैं तुम्हे अपनी डायरी में लिखती हूँ।

1) हर की पौड़ी....

जलती धूप की खिलती खुशबू में मंदिरों की घंटी बजती है , द्रीप जलते
ऐसे मानो यह शाखा कैलाशी है , ऐसी पौड़ी देखी जिसमे धरता पाव
स्वर्ग पर
हो , जैसे जैसे कदम बढ़े यह हर की पौड़ी हो .,

2) बेखबर

कुछ ख़यालो से बेखबर यह विचार मेरा , नए खयाल बुनकर पुराने उधेड़ता है।

3) काश ये मौसम.....

काश ये मौसम रह ही जाए सुबह यही, शाम यही और यह रात मेरा यहां होना , तेरा यहां होना हमारी ये बातें , यही लड़ाईया ,यही प्यार काश ये मौसम रह ही जाए ....इस बार.

4) चाय से जुड़ा एक किस्सा याद है..

माँ के हाथ की बनी चाय आज भी बहोत खास है जब पहली बार स्वाद लिया था उस चाय का जो माँ ने बनाई थी तब से ही तोह शौक़ हुआ जो आज भी बरकरार है।

Poonam Naik

Poonam Naik is 20 year old B.scB.Ed student at Ganpat Parsekar College of Education Harmal Goa. I am from panjim City of Goa. Recently I have started writing poems in that I like to share my daily life experiences and love for my family, society, and respect to country.

वतन से बढ़कर कुछ और नहीं

सरहद पर खड़े रहकर
देश की हिफाज़त करते हैं।
ऊंची ऊंची पहाड़ियों पर
वतन को गगन में लहराते हैं।

मौत को सामने देखकर
अपने कदम कभी पीछे नहीं लेते हैं।
सरहद पर कुर्बानियां देकर
वतन के खातिर शहीद होते हैं।

सीने में गोलियां लेकर
गहरी जख्म भी सहते हैं।
मगर कभी दुश्मनों से हार नहीं मानते
और वतन के खातिर
आखिरी सांस तक लड़ते हैं।

न कभी बर्फ की थंड लगती है।
और न ही रेगिस्तान की गर्मी
महसूस होती है।
दिल में वतन की इज्जत और
हिपगड़ाता से बढ़कर
जान की भी फिक्र नहीं होती है।

मेरे प्यारे पापा

एक लड़की को संभालते- संभालते
लड़ते रहे वह पूरी दुनिया से।
मुझे रख दिया छांव में और
खुद जलते रहे कड़ी धूप में।

मेरे सपनों का ख्याल रखते-रखते
खुद के सपने भी भूल गए।
मुझे ख़ुशीया देते-देते
मेरी खुशीयों में अपनी खुशियां ढूंढते रहे।

बचपन से ही हाथ पकड़कर आये
और बुरे वक्त में भी साथ देते रहे।
यह पापा का प्यार ही है जो
एक बेटी का दोस्त बन गए।

बेटी की आंखों में आसूं आयें तो
पापा की आंखें दर्द महसूस करती है।
और बेटी की आंखें खुशियों से भरें
तो पापा भी ख़ुश हो जातें हैं।

जिनके आंगन में बेटी हैं
उनका आंगन कभी सुना नहीं होता।
और जिन के पास पापा जैसे दोस्त हों
उनके जिंदगी में किसी की कमी नहीं होती।

औरतों को इज्जत देना सीखों

औरत अपनी जिम्मेदारियां संभालते- संभालते
अपनी खुशियां कुर्बान कर देती है।
यहां तक कि शादी के बाद
अपना मायका छोड़कर
ससुराल जाती है।

परिवार में कभी दरारें न आए
इसलिए सारा दोष अपने सीर पर लेती है।
यहां तक कि बड़ों के ताने सुनते- सुनते
घर से बाहर निकलना भी बंद कर देती है।

औरत को अगर इज्जत देना सीख गए
तो घर में कभी मां, बहन या बेटीयां
मूसिबत में नहीं मिलेगी।
औरत ना हीं कमजोर है और
ना हीं गवार अगर उसका
थोड़ा-सा हौसला बढ़ाओंगे और साथ दोगे
तो वह हर घर का नाम रौशन करेंगी।

मोहब्बत की कुर्बानी

मोहब्बत हो गई थी उनसे
मगर तकदीर के आगे झुक गए हम।
सात साल साथ रहकर भी
तनहाई जैसे बिछड़ गए हम।

सफर में मिलें थे वह उन्हें हमसफ़र
बनाना चाहती थी मगर
लाचार, बेबस होकर अपने
प्यार को खो दिया मैंने।

जब तक जिंदगी है तब तक साथ रहेंगे
ऐसा वादा किया था एक-दूसरे से
मगर मां-पापा की खुशीयों के खातिर
अपने मोहब्बत को भुला दिया मैंने।

उन्हें झूठ के अंधेरे में
रखना नहीं चाहतीं थीं इसलिए
खुद को उनके काबिल न होने का
एहसास दिलाकर अपनी मोहब्बत को
खो दिया हम ने।

बचपन

कौन कहता है सबका बचपन
अच्छा होता है।
जहां पेट भर खाना नहीं
वहां बच्चा भी मजदूर होता है।

जिन हाथों में कलम देना चाहिए
उन हाथों में बंदूक थमायी जाती है।
जिन कंधों पर किताबों का दफ्तर होना चाहिए
उन कंधों पर जिम्मेदारियां दी जाती है।

कौन कहता है सबका बचपन
अच्छा होता है।
जिन बच्चों के मां बाप नहीं
उन बच्चों का तो बचपन ही
चला जाता है।

Gaurangi Mishra

Gaurangi Mishra is 13 yrs old . She's a student. She is a blank verse and a gothic writer. She believesthat a writer is a person who can put his thoughts, acts , feelings and desires with power of pen. She wil keep on writing on new goals n desires that everyone carries while climbing life with ups n downs.

Alone

A word he fears the most but a word he is used to
Alone
It has always been like that, he doesn't know what to do
Forsaken by his mother
Hated by his father
Abandoned by a sister & a brother
Unwillingly ruined into a monster
Strong & immortal, he wanders the earth
Forever imprisoned, forever under a curse
Surrounded by comrades, but never a friend
Tortured, longing for it all to end
Longing for a father's love
For a mother's care
For a brotherly hug
Longing to have someone to share
His life with, it would've been enough
Instead, there's hatred & rage
Forever a monster entrapped in eternity's cage.
Alone.
He has a face a world that hates him.
Alone.
Everyone even his, family wants to kill him
But in spite of this all.
Alone is where he belongs.
Because the winner stands alone
To be a winner he longs...

Far Away From The World Apart

I want to fly away like a bird;
Higher and higher.
Above in the sky;
Far away from the world apart.

Where nobody goes;
Where society full of cruelty doesn't exist.
Where falling apart isn't a crime;
Where no paths are needed to be followed.

I want to fly away with my wings open;
Like a bird higher and higher.
Above in the sky;
Far away from the world apart.
Where the world is not like a trap;
Where wings aren't clipped and toes aren't tied.
Where dreams are seen but society isn't mean;

Where life isn't ruled;
And paths aren't followed but created!!

Wanna Fly?

I want to fly away into this sky,
To anywhere I please.
That glitter in the sky?
I want to scoop it all up in my hands.

Damn you gravity!
But I can't let you win this time.
'Cause I just want to get away like a bird,
And let my spirit fly in all degrees...
SO DON'T TELL ME TO WALK;
WHEN I WANT TO FLY!!

Do You Believe

My heart is weak, the soul is deep with words I can speak. But would you listen, understand or even believe?! So I prefer to show in actions; Take you on a journey of my thoughts' So when words are spoken, Then the walls are broken. And you believe in my love; Because my heart is weak, my soul is deep with the words I can speak.....

Nightmare Child

It ain't funny, it ain't pretty, it ain't sweet. I hear it at night, it growls at me I   have my back facing it but I know it's crawlin' At me, into me. It's a quiet noise, Even when its right next to me, almost silent. I can feel it wrapping me and everything that I hold.

Garvita Mishra

Garvita Mishra is 14 years old. She's a student . She is enthusiastic n creative writer . She enjoys writing to brighten young minds with delight n new energy feeling. She believe to refresh each with new feelings with her pen movements.

Child Of Cosmos

There will always be a universe in my mind;
With full of meteorites and comets.
As I want stars, strength all balance in my soul.
Doesn't it look somewhat demonic?
The sky is so tragically beautiful,
A graveyard of stars.
And even look at the moon being so dutiful.
Cause it has its own scars.
Each one of us quickly grows,
As the river flows,
With so many sorrows and woes,
Looks like we are all survivors of the cosmos.....

Dry Dust

I was smelling dust,
Flowers on the graveyard going pale and rust.
Felt the sense of cold air.
Everyone was packed in a layer.
Warmth was never cup of my tea.
Taking everything apart.
I stood and I watch.
Everything falling into pieces,
And no-one else to pick up.
Strange darkness pulled us all in.
Just ashes, bones and skin...

More Stars More Me

I want to fly,
Get the approach high;
Let you, puke in the sky.
Oh, love, come the way you are.
Let us, no worry for this pretty night,
Come forth and feel the star;
Everything, I sight, I think you might like.
For now I'm pleading;
To stop this heart from bleeding.
From their no tomorrow;
And from here forget all sorrow,
Ah, come the stars, I want to feel you,
'Cause from now I think, there is only you.
I don't want to sleep down by the skies,
'Cause there are only the shadows of lies;
With some crows wearing some fascinating ties.
Release this chains,
'Cause, I wanna feel the rain;
Like an underneath grain.
Get away this thing called loner,
Don't want to be more than a mourner.
I don't know how to tie my laces,
How to solve this so-called rigid cases?;
But I know how to run from the life's races.
'Cause, I've my own master dazzling stars;
So, I can wash away my dirty scars....

She Can't

Inside she's a wreck,
When you see her she looks perfectly fine,
Deep down her mind is a mess;
When she's with you she looks happy.
But she's alone; fragile.
The girl with broken dreams; defeated by destiny.
She wants to escape, from the people around.
To a city unknown;
And perhaps one day,
When you ask her, "are you fine?"
For once she'll say, "I'm fine."
And it wouldn't.
Be a lie.
She really can't fight this battle,
But deep down she knows, she has to.
A girl with a heart and full of pain inside it;
No matter what, she has to accept that she's vulnerable.
Every time people try to play with her feelings, mind, and
heart;
But from outside, she looks like it doesn't matter the girl at all.
From inside she feels it and become overwhelmed;
She can't fight this anymore and moving in oblivion..

Nothing Stand By Her Side

She cried, cried and cried,
for everyone whom she's sired.
Even her heart is doomed and tired.

Her love and gratitude for someone,
her possession and caring;
But she knows that it is not long lasting.

Everything just depends on her one pill,
but, even it's making herself going downhill.

She wants to be free and happy,
and, wants to forget her past.
But it's also not last.

Showing herself an exuberant.
Showing herself an extrovert.
But who knows she's all alone from inside and has left with a
little bit hope.

MAKING HERSELF LOPE...

Saumya Agrawal

"Saumya" The name itself reflects the warmth, She is as calm as moon, being a third person to write about her is an opportunity to let m t heart speaks about her. She is a girl full of love and care, She carries a child inside her heart to get all the joy around, She carries a women insideher heart to feel the reality of the society. Girl full of great thoughts andinnovative ideas to roam around, an upcoming bright writter she is.   Let her shine, Let her be the new face of your inner thoughts.

त्याग ही जीवन हैं

मनुष्य के जीवन मे उनको बिना त्याग के कुछ नहीं मिलता है।

हम मनुष्य सुबह जब उठते है, तब से ले कर, रात मे जब बिस्तर पे जाते है, हम जो भी करते उनमें त्याग की भूमिका बहुत अहम होती है।

बहुत मुश्किल से कोई अपनी जिंदगी खुद से अपने लिए जीता है, नहीं तो लोग त्याग ही करते करते अपने जीवन को बिता देते है।

पुरुष और औरत दोनो अपने जीवन मे बहुत त्याग करते है ।

पुरुषों को लगता है त्याग केवल हम पुरुष करते है,और औरतों को लगता है त्याग केवल हम औरत करते है,लेकिन ऐशा नहीं होता ,दोनों अपनी अपनी जगह त्याग करते है।

हम इंसान कब अपनो के लिए त्याग कर देते है इसका हमे खुद एहसास नहीं होता। और सबसे शान्ति तब मिलती है जब हम किसी अंजान दूसरे इंसान के लिए त्याग करते है जिनको बहुत जरूरत होती है हमारे मदद की लेकिन वो हमे कह नहीं सकते।

जिंदगी में बिना त्याग किए आपको एक सुई भी नहीं मिलेगी।

 त्याग ही जीवन हैं

पापा आप के बिना हम कुछ नहीं

पापा आप के बिना हम कुछ नहीं,
हमें जब भी किसी चीज़ कि जरुरत होती है आप हमेशा उसको पुरा करते है,
आप कितने भी परेशान रहे लेकिन कभी दिखाते नहीं है,
अपनी परिवार के लिए पुरी जान दे देते है आप,
खुद के लिए कभी कुछ नहीं करते लेकिन हम सब के लिए हमेशा करते है|
पापा आप के बिना हम कुछ नहीं,
पापा आप है तो हमारा परिवार है क्युकि आप सब चीज़ इतनी सरलता से हैंडल करते है,
पापा आप पुरे दिन काम कर के आने के बाद भी कभी ये नहीं महसूस करते है कि आप थक गए है,
आज तक आप ने कभी अपने लिए कुछ नहीं सोचा है।
पापा आप के बिना हम कुछ नहीं,
बहुत चीज़ ऐसी होती है पापा जो आपका मन नहीं होता है लेकिन अपनों के लिए आप ख़ुशी ख़ुशी सब कर देते है,
हम सब कि सारी जिद हमेशा पुरी करते है,
पापा आप ही हमारी पुरी दुनिया है|

दोस्ती..

एक अनोखा रिश्ता, दो अजनबी लोग अलग परिवार, लेकिन दोस्तो की बाद अपनो से भी बढ़ के हो जाती हैं।सच्चे दोस्त वो होते है जो कभी गलत नहीं चाहते अपने दोस्तों का।कभी कभी उनको पता होता है कि वो जो बोलेंगे, उस से उनका दोस्त उदास होगा ,लेकिन एक पल कि ख़ुशी के लिए गलत नहीं बोलेंगे आप के दोस्त।सच्चे दोस्त आप के दुःख मे आप के साथ दुःखी होंगे और आप के सुख मे आप के साथ खुश होंगे।जरुरी नहीं है कि दोस्ती हमेशा पास रह के निभाया जाए अगर आपको दोस्ती निभानी हैं,आप दुनिया के किसी भी कोने मे रहकर निभा सकते हैं।सच्चे दोस्त आपसे कितना भी दूर क्यों ना रहते हो लेकिन दिल के बहुत करीब रहते हैं।एक सच्चे दोस्त को लोग अपने जिंदगी की हर एक बात बता सकता हैं।आप जब दुःखी होंगे तो एक सच्चा दोस्त ही होता हैं जो आपको खुश करने कि हर एक कोशिश करता हैं। और जब तक वो सफल नहीं होता वो मानता नहीं।

जीवन एक संघर्ष हैं।

हम सभी के लिए जीवन में अलग अलग लक्ष्य होते है।जैसे किसी का लक्ष्य स्कूल या कॉलेज में टॉप करना,किसी का लक्ष्य अच्छा बिजनेस खड़ा करना होता हैं।तो हर एक व्यक्ति अपने अपने क्षेत्र में कामयाब होना चाहता हैं।लेकिन कामयाबी उन्ही को मिलती हैं जो संघर्ष के लिए तैयार होता हैं।वैसे तो संघर्ष और इंसान का रिश्ता पैदा होने से पहले से चालू हो जाता हैं।और पैदा होने के बाद दो पांव पे चलने के लिए भी संघर्ष ही करना होता हैं। सब लोग अलग अलग तरह से संघर्ष करते हैं, कभी अपनों के लिए और कभी खुद के लिए।क्लास में अच्छे नंबर लाने के लिए संघर्ष ,इसके बाद कॉलेज या बिजनेस या खेल या किसी में कामयाबी पाने के लिए संघर्ष करना पड़ता हैं।इसके बाद शादी फिर परिवार फिर परिवार की जरूरतों को पूरा करने का संघर्ष ।

इसी को कहते हैं संघर्ष ।

निम्र सोच

दुनिया मे बहुत तरह के लोग हैं, सबकी सोच अलग अलग है लेकिन मैं यहा लड़का लड़की के बीच अंतर करने वाले लोगों के बारे में अपनी विचार रख रही|पहले लोग लड़कियों के पैदा होने से पहले ही उसे गर्भ में मार देते थे क्योंकि उनको लड़का चाहिए होता था।आज भी बहुत जगह ऐसा होता है लेकिन धीरे धीरे लोगों कि सोच बदल गई हैं| बहुत लोग लड़कियों को पढ़ना भी नहीं चाहते है क्योंकि उनको लगता है लड़कियों को पढ़ना मतलब पैसा बर्बाद। पराई घर की धन है, पराए घर चली जाएगी तो क्या करे पढ़ा के। लड़कियों से सिर्फ चूल्हा चौका का काम सिखाते है।क्यों लड़कियों का अपने जिवन पर अधिकार नही हैं? उनको हमेशा दूसरों के हिसाब से क्यों चलना पड़ता हैं? पहले मां बाप, फिर सास ससुर पति, फिर बच्चें। इसी में जिंदगी निकल जाती है उनकी।बहुत लोग लड़कियों कि शादी छोटी उम्र मे कर देते है क्योंकि उनको लगता हैं लड़कियाँ उनके लिए बोझ हैं|लड़कियों का अपना कोई घर नहीं होता हैं शादी से पहले सुनती है तुमको पराए घर जाना हैं और शादी के बाद सुनती है तुम तो पराए घर से आई हो|पता नहीं लोग इतनी नीच सोच क्यों रखते हैं लड़कियों के प्रति? हमेसा हर जगह लड़कियों को ही झुकना क्यों पड़ता हैं ।

Prakriti Garg

She is prakriti Garg..she is basically belongs to rewa city of Madhya Pradesh.she was graduated in BE..CSE...form RGPV.... university Bhopal.....she is a great writer and poetess.. She wants childhood method should be adopting on a new platform....

Insta id:-.. prakriti 3507

ज़रा ठहरो

ज़रा ठहरो
तुम गद्दारों, गद्दारी की सीख मिली है।
सीखो तो, कुछ हमसे भी।
हम नही तब भी, आग हर दिलों में जली है।
बुझ गए चिराग़, बदल गए हालात,
टूट गए सपने, बिखर गए अपने।
आंखें नम और ली है कसम।
खून के बदले खून

वजूद

कुछ वक्त के लिए दूर हो सकता है।
पर भूल नही सकता है।
यकीन है,
मुझे अपने वजूद पर।

शिक्षक

तेरी शरण में आए, तो तुमने सब समझाया,
भला बुरा पता न मुझको, तुमने है बतलाया।
राह भटक गए तो, तुमने है दिखलाया,
चाहत है कुछ पाने की , मन में विश्वास जगाया !!
क्या मांगू अब तुझसे, आशीष बनाए रखना,
आशा है बस इतनी, विश्वास बनाए रखना,
था जीवन अंधेरे में, तुमने प्रकाश है लाया।
कैसे आभार मानू आपका, जो अद्भुत ज्ञान दिलाया।

ख्वाहिशों की कशमकश

ख्वाहिशों की कशमकश में,
कोशिश ही नही करते खुद को आजमाने की,
ए जिंदगी
एक भी वजह तू बता दे,
मेरे मुस्कुराने की।

है ज़िंदगी

है ज़िंदगी
उस राह पर
जहां ख्वाहिश तो बदलती है
मगर
ख्वाब आज भी कहीं न कहीं जिंदा है !!

(6)

Chahiye .....
Sirf sukoon.....
Tujhse.....
Aye Zindagi....
Aur kch v nhi...

Sonia Chhabra

Sonia chhabra titles

1 president of mission smile ngo, 2.dazzling diva mrs.india continent2018, 3.mrs.north india talented 2017, 4.mrs.punjabn 2nd runner up dec.2017, 5.mrs.royal ldh .jan 2018, 6.ms.jugni 2017, 7.winner super mom & kid show . 2014, 8.mrs.teej queen..2017, 9. Pride of ldh 2018, 10.elite face of india 2018, 11. National women excellence award 2018 , 12.volunteer of ngo named ek noor sewa kendar   , 13.dazzling diva face of india 2018, 14.prtibhashali punjabn , 15.brand ambassador of kohinoor mrs.world punjabn 2018 & 2019, 16.super dynamic women 2019, 17.queen of universe , 18.gidyan di rani , 19..mrs.universe asia international 2019 , 20 stunning diva of india 2019, 21 style icon of who , 22 women excellence award 2019

कुर्बानी

वक्त और हालात
मांग रहे आज कुरबानी
चाहिये आज लोगों में जोश की रवानी
मास्क ,सैनिटाइजर और
सोशल डिस्टनसिंग से ही
पड़ेगी अपनी जान बचानी
हिम्मत और हौंसलों से ही
आगे बढ़ेगी कहानी
सोनिया कहे...
रख होंसला वो समय भी आएगा
कोरोना को मात देकर
खिला खिला हर चेहरा नज़र आएगा
अपने सपनों की उड़ान
हर कोई भर पाएगा
जीत जाएगा ये जहाँ
हर कोई गुनगुनयेगा
हर कोई गुनगुनयेगा

रिश्ते

रिश्तों की कीमत नहीं होती
रिश्ते कीमती हैं होते
यह हैं वो एहम रिश्ते
जिनसे एहसास अपनों के होते
इनसे ही होती खुशियाँ
इनसे ही मौज मस्ती के मेले होते
पर आजकल रिश्ते बदल रहे हैं
अपने ही अपनों को गिरा रहे हैं
खून भी पानी बन रहे हैं
समय नहीं किसी के पास रिश्ते निभाने को
बस अपनी ही धुन और अपने लिए ही जी रहे हैं
सोनिया कहे.....
वक़्त रहते रिश्ते सम्भाल लो
रूठ गए अपनों को मना लो
न जाने कब कोई अपना छूट जाए
इन बेशक़ीमती हीरों को सम्भाल लो
क्योंकि जीवन की डोर बड़ी कमज़ोर

रिश्तों को निभाने के लिए

रिश्तों को निभाने के लिए
बहुत कुछ सहना पड़ता है
मांगती है कुर्बानी
हर औरत की कहानी
सब रिश्तों को उसे ही समेटना पड़ता है
अपनों की खुशियों के लिये
अपना हर आंसू उसे छुपाना पड़ता है
धूप में ठंडी छाँव बनकर
तो कभी आसमाँ बन कर
अपना आँचल उसे फैलाना पड़ता है
सोनिया कहे....
अपना वजूद भुलाकर हर रिश्ता निभाती है
हर रूप रंग में जो ढल जाती है
सलाम है हर उस औरत को
जो खुद के सपने मार कर
अपने घर को स्वर्ग बनातीं है
अपने घर को स्वर्ग बनाती है

मुस्कुराहट

मुस्कुराहट का कोई
मोल नहीं होता
एक छोटी सी मुस्कुराहट
पे दिल है खिलता
मुस्कुराता चेहरा सब को
सुकून है देता
उदास मन की भी दवा है बनता
हँसते मुस्कुराते काट लो
ज़िन्दगी के रास्ते
किसी के चेहरे की
मुस्कान बन जाओ
या जी लो किसी के वास्ते
सोनिया कहे......
हर मुश्किल,हर गम की दवा है मुस्कान
खिलखिलाते चेहरों की पहचान है मुस्कान
चलो मिल कर छोटी सी मुस्कुराहटें बाँटे
चलो मिल कर दिलों से नफ़रतें छांटे

काश ऐसा हो जाए

हर तरफ खुशी हो
गमों से हर कोई दूर हो
दिल किसी का कोई तोड़े न
अपनों से कोई मुँह मोड़े न
नफ़रतों के कोई बीज बोए न
नीचा गिराने की कोई होड़ होए न
आदमी ही आदमी से डरे न
इंसानियत का धर्म कोई छोड़े न
प्यार ही प्यार हो हर जगह
किसी की आंख से आंसू आये न
सोनिया कहे......
गर ऐसा हो जाये
तो जिंदगी जन्नत हो जाये
गर ऐसा हो जाये
तो यहीं सब को स्वर्ग मिल जाये
गर ऐसा हो जाये
तो हर कोई इस प्यार की
दौलत से धनवान हो जाये
काश ऐसा हो जाये
काश ऐसा हो जाये

Rajeshwari Chaubey

Passionate hard work takes a person to the highest peak of success.
She is a girl having dreams in her eyes and a passion to write,let me present miss Rajeshwari chaubey whose continuous efforts to win all your hearts are adding up day by day.She is a very beautiful writer whose words will take you to the world of words.Hope you all will like her writeups.
All your love and support is needed.

Sacrifices Are Made

Sacrifices are made but are never meant.
You all have sacrificed something at some point of life,either for a relationship or for your dreams.
Sacrifice simply means to pay for what you want to get and the more you offer the more you gain.Can you recall a relationship which lasted long and the reason why?
Let me answer this for you, every relationship has i   ts own circumstances and it runs by its own way but there are some common factors on which these relations depend are understanding, adjustment, acceptance and sacrifice.If the two person are in relationship and they understand each other,accept and respect each other's opinion than it is a healthy relationship.But every relationship demands sacrifices as it is not necessary that you will get the perfect match of Your expectations,thus you need to accept this fact and it's consequences too.
And the relationship in which there is no place for sacrifice than it slowly turns into an unhealthy one or will end up giving you lot of regrets.

To Nurture Your Bond

To nurture your bond with your loved ones
Sometimes You need to offer them without caring of your own happiness.
Its in human nature that whenever they do something for someone they expect appreciation.But as it is said if you are helping someone than don't expect anything in return, similarly when you are doing any sacr   ifice for your loved one,may you don't get the expected response but that does not make your work worthless.If what you did is the reason of someone's smile today than even if it is not considered you should be happy and kind hearted.
Therefore, sacrifices are necessary but not significantly for a relationship.It plays a very vital role in your life when it comes to your dreams, sacrifices are very much important in achieving your goals and in accomplishing your dreams.
Remember,if you are not ready to pay   for it,than you will definitely not get it. Nothing comes for free not even your dreams,they also demand sacrifices.
To pursue your dreams you need to focus on your goal and to focus you need to cut all the distractions from your mind.Even if it is the most lovely thing of yours,if it is the cost than you have to pay it.

Love-A Sacrifice

I still remember how it begun
When for the first time
I felt for him
I still can't tell what was special about him
But there was nothing in him
That doesn't attracted me
With my full power
I tried not to fall for him
But whenever I looked into his eyes
I forgot anything happening around me
I tried every single thing to stop me
But I failed to and decided to go on with him
The beauty of his love was
There were no promises made
There was only term and condition
To love each other the best way
He never asked me
Where was I going and why
He always gave me a trusted vibe
We thought we will live happily ever after
But the destiny has decided something else
The happiness in our bond and the love between us was to be
shattered
And as we separated the rumours spread
And with this spread misunderstandings increased
And it finally took us to the end
The sacrifices we made has no meaning now
But our love was there and will be there
Even if we are alive or after life.

He Sacrificed Me

He sacrificed me,as he paid his feelings,as a cost of his dreams

He motivated the whole world, but the irony is,he destroyed his own heart.

Abhinaya Reddy

Abhinaya Reddy Abhieshu, The writer. Life means that the way of leaving according to her. She believes that she born to become author.

Mail :- Reddyabhinaya328@Gmail.com

Sacrifice Of A Mother

To know the value of a birth is to experience it.
To know the value of a life is to give a birth to someone.
To know the value of a mind one must understand the mom.
As well as wanting to know the value of a mom must and should know the secrifice of mom for a child.
In this whole universe no one else can make the sacrifice that mom can makes for us.
So moms are treated as visible goddess because of her unspeakable sacrifice.

Sacrifice Of A Soldier

Today we the people here are living peacefully without any fear of Britishers means the greatness of the sogldiers only but also the soldier's family.
So please respect soldiers and their families.

Sacrifice Of A Friend

A friend, who really sacrifice fo r you what you need without any problem then you feel that person is really your true friend and don't miss that friend unnecessarily.
Because true relations doesn't comes again. They only come once in a lifetime.

Mehtaz Nasrin Ahmed

Mehtaz Nasrin Ahmed is a writer and a poet by passion. She is an M. Sc in Applied Geology and an active participant of the 4th South Asian Geoscience Conference, GeoINDIA 2018.She loves travelling places, observe the exposures, find the geology in it and taste the traditions of different localities. The vast experiences of her travel, people, culture, food and nature has always led her question different opinions on the subject and she chosed to pen down her thoughts that pop up in her mind. In this way she has a   gathered collection of her penned down thoughts in different platforms such as in 'Your Quote'.

Love and Sacrifice

Aneeta was born to a middle class family in a village situated at the outskirts of Udaipur. Her father was a small buisnessman and her mother, a homemaker. She was the only child of her parents. Her father's monthly income was just enough to serve the family. Aneeta during her childhood was able to secure good in her academics . She was also apt in some other skills like singing and writing. She grew up as a modest Indian girl and started learning her school and skills thoroughly. Soon she was able to win every school held competition in singing.

Her mother started to find out ways to earn more to give her best training for her skills and studies. Aneeta's mother started a tea-stall in front of their home and started earning little through it. Besides these she had to manage her small farm and family. Aneeta then started taking up different district level and national level competitions in singing. She was equally acheiving heights in her academic record. Gradually the expenditure for Aneeta's education and training started to increase and at some point it was not affordable and unbearable by her parents. Aneeta's mother sold off all her jewe lleries in order to pay Aneeta's graduation coursefee. Aneeta took honors in Psychology and could complete her graduation securing first class 1st rank from her college. She eventually got admitted to Mumbai University for her masters. This time Aneeta could bear her own expenses through her merit Scholarship. Since her University was far from her hometown, she could hardly make a visit to her home in a year.

Aneeta was a well practising psychology student and an active participant in different national and international conferences. She has earned different awards,fame and attained heights through her great work. Her parents were very happy for her   . After two years of consistent effort Aneeta could complete her masters with flying colours. She eventually got an offer to work in University of Texas and started her career as a phd Research Scholar in Department of Psychology, University of

Texas.Aneeta wasproud to be a part of Texas family and her parents were proud of her.

She started her PhD coursework and could get her project funded within six months and started working for a paper. While she was busy in her research and analysis work, one day she got a phone call from her father informing her about her mother's ill health. She got to know that her mother was suffering from blood cancer and the doctor has given her only a year survival time. Her father was too old to take care of her mother. Aneeta was deeply saddened by the news and finally decided to leave her PhD in Texas and go back to her home and take care of her mother. Aneeta's homecoming was a great strength to her parents mentally while it was a question mark to her career. She started working in a school in her locality and took care of her mother's health in a top superspeciality hospital. She stayed with her, spent hours and sleepless nights helping her breathe and stay happy. She was a support system to her father too.
In this way Aneeta took care of her mother and she stayed happily for 9 months and then one day while Aneeta was helping her mother have lunch, her mother started coughing and couldn't stop. She breathed for the last time leaving Aneeta and her father in tears.
Few days after her mother's cremation, Aneeta was informed by her guide from Texas that her small research work in the beginning of her research work got published in an international journal and is having a good number of citations.
Aneeta who was deeply mourne d by her mother's death was surprised to hear this news and felt really happy. She was then offered to work as a Lecturer in Texas University. She initially denied the offer since her father was at his old age and there was none other than her to look after him. But after checking out the provisions of her and her father's stay in Texas, she had decided to take her father alongwith her and continue with her profession in Texas

Ritu Sachdeva

Ritu Sachdeva is Director of Ritzcoaching path to success. is a certified life and wellness coach with a work experience of 15 years

Kurban

A small town girl
Sacrifice is not only when you sacrifice for your family or any one close to you.
At times sacrifice is also to sacrifice our own self for our dreams and aspirations.
Once there was a small -town girl. Who use to stay in a small town , she never knew what the other side world looks like or how was the life of big cities or town and than there comes a day when she
She had to attend her cousins marriage in one of the cities and finally she reaches there along with her family members and when she was exposed to that life she was very much attracted towards the life in cities. She was so awestruck that she decided to leave her small town and settle down there.
With the concern and permission of her family she decided to pursue her dreams in the city.
And one day she was their. Being born and bought up in small town it was not that easy or our STG(small town girl)to adjust in that environment .From dressing to   talking style , from thinking pattern to be politically correct , everything seems a new challenge . Struggling to adjust and a be someone who she was not was a great challenge and needed her to sacrifice many things to be someone who she actually is not .Trying to adjust in the so called city life our STG lost her true self
She became successful and did whatever she wanted .She was the most success full in her field with a complete emptiness in her as she lost her true self in trying to achieve her dreamsand reaching at the top of her career.
IT is not only about STG it about all of us wherein we loss ourselves trying to achieve our dreams or trying to being with someone ,trying to adjust with the families after marriage some where each and every girls sacrifices and losses her true self trying to adjust .

If you are in office talk like this , dress like this .If you are in public place dress like this behave like this, if you are married forget what your mother taught and adjust to the standard of that family. And when you are a mother forget about yourself and look after your children .

If you move from one city to another talk and behave certain way .

Why there are so many sacrifices in every scenario of life .Why we loss ourself always in this rat race   of society why every time we need to do some or the other kurbani for the sake of society standards and to be right as set by others .

Divya Nokhwal

She is Divya nokhwal daughter of Vinod Kumar.
She is Science student.

कुछ अल्फ़ाज़ महोब्बत के नाम

रहने को बहुत जगह है जमाने में
पर हमे घर भी तेरे दिल में चाहिए
हम इंतजार कर रहे हैं जो तेरी महोंबत का
हमे वो सबर भी तेरे दिल में चाहिए
जो तलाश कर रही है तेरी खुशियां , ये मेरी नजर
हमे वो नजर भी तेरे दिल में चाहिए
मेरे लिए कीमती है तेरा हर अल्फ़ाज़
हमें ये कदर भी तेरे दिल में चाहिए
किस हाल मे हूं मै तेरे बिना
हमे ये खबर भी तेरे दिल में चाहिए
है जिंदगी जब तक , मेरी रूह को महोबत है तुझसे
और मौत के बाद
मुझे मेरी कब्र भी तेरे दिल में चाहिए

तारीफ़_ए_महबूब

उसके चेहरे पर काली जुल्फ़े
जैसे चांद पर बदलो का पहरा है
वो निकले जब काला लिबास पहन कर
जैसे निकला रात को सवेरा है
उसके कदमों की आहट
जैसे बिजली ने राग छेड़ा है
उसके पायल की छनकार
जैसे बिन मौसम बदलो ने सावन घेरा है
उसके बातो की खनक
जैसे दूर तालाब में बूंदे गिरी है
उसके आंखो का काजल
जैसे सूरज के चारो ओर अंधेरा है
उसके होठों की हसी
दम निकाल दे मुर्दो का
जिसकी हर अदा है जहर सी कातिल
ऐसा महबूब मेरा है

स्कूल की याद

सिर्फ़ तू ही नहीं थी स्कूल में
फिर भी तुझसे दिल लगाया मैंने
सब जानते थे तेरा नाम मेरी क्लास मे
फिर भी यारो को तेरा नाम बताया मैंने
सब खबर थी मेरे घर पर मेरे बारे में
फिर भी तेरा जिक्र उनसे छिपाया मैंने
लिखकर तेरा नाम किसी मेज पर
मेरे जिगरी को दिखाया मैने
निकल कर स्कूल से तेरे घर तक
दूर से ही सही ,तुझे तेरे घर तक पहुंचाया मैंने
किसी रोज सबसे छुपाकर अपनी कलाई पर
तेरे नाम का पहला अक्षर खुदवाया मैने
मिन्नतों पर मांग कर बाईक किसी यार की
हर शाम तेरी गली का चक्कर लगाया मैने
वो भी क्या दिन थे स्कूल के
जब तेरी छोटी सी खुशी को खुद से ज्यादा बताया मैने

वक्त निकाल मेरे लिए

मै तपती जमीन सा
मुझे तेरी बारिश का इंतजार
थोड़ा वक्त निकाल मेरे लिए
देख मुझे तुझसे कितना है प्यार
मै बिना खुश्बू का फूल हूं
तू है नए मौसम की बहार
थोड़ा वक्त निकाल मेरे लिए
मुझे है तेरा बेसब्री से इंतजार
ये दुनिया पसन्द नहीं मुझको
तेरी खुशियों मे खुश है मेरा परिवार
थोड़ा वक्त निकाल मेरे लिए
तू ही है मेरा छोटा सा संसार
मेरी आंखे है वो आइना
जिसे पसन्द है सिर्फ़ तेरा दीदार
थोड़ा वक्त निकाल मेरे लिए
मै हू तेरी दुरियो से बीमार

महोबत पर सितम

मेरा दर्द तेरे जख्मों से ख़तम होने लगा
मेरी ज़िन्दगी तेरे ज़हर पर जीने लगी
तेरी कैद मुझे रिहाई से भी ज्यादा पसन्द आ रही हैं
तेरे जुल्म की हवा मुझे सुकून देने लगी
तू जिस आग में छोड़ गई अब वहां भी ठंड लगती है
ये तेरी इश्क से नफ़रत मेरे दिल में बसती है
तेरी याद अब काफी नहीं मेरे लिए
तेरी कमी जिस्म में पानी सी खलती है
ये जो दिन_ब_दिन तू सितम हम पर ढा रही है
इन्हे सह कर हमारी महोबत अंगारों सी जलती है
तेरी नजर से रूबरू होने को मेरी रूह
इस जिस्म के पिंजरे में मचलती हैं
तू ज़रा हम पर गौर करके देख तो सही
मेरी महोबत तेरी नफ़रत से दस कदम आगे चलती हैं

Sureka Velusamy

She is Sureka velusamy. She is studying 11th standard .She is doing her studies in RKV Matric Higher Secondary School. She is living at Namakkal in Tamilnadu .She has started her writing journey from her 8th standard. This is her first book in which she is working as a co author She is an Indian .She will write in two languages Tamil and English .She is interested in writing poems, quotes and short stories.She wanted to become a great writer in her future.She's the one who says that
EVEN MY DEATH IS WAITING
I'LL NEVER STOP MY WRITING.

The First Sacrificer

Once a farmer lived in a village with his family. They are very poor family. Actually he belongs to a rich family but he is poor because his family members didn't accept them to do agriculture . So they sacrificed everything and came out without anything to become a farmer. He came out and stayed in his friends house and got a land for rent and started to farm. He got married and have two children.He married a blind woman. He sacrificed his whole life for her.They are very poor now.They don't even know wha t to do for the next meal. In the past there was a flood and crops in the field had lost in that.He got a loan and planted once again with confidence. The days passed slowly. Six months passed in the poverty.

The Day To Harvest

The day to harvest had come.The world had completely locked down. So he couldn't harvest. The world had changed completely .He had only his own house in which he is living now.He sacrificed many things .He sacrifices the food that he eats because the will not enough for his childr en.Many days he slept in hunger.Now the person who gave loan has started to ask the money back.Slowly the world is coming out of the lockdown. The government had brought in three new laws for farmers which the farmers dont like.The farmers protested against the law for nearly 150 days but the government didn't get back the law.Even they're not ready to hear the problems of the farmers. He don't know what to do.

He Decided To Leave

He decided to leave the world.This decision had taken by him only for his family.He wanted to make his children a great person so he wanted to make them study.He don't even have food for next meal.How will he make   them study.If he died they'll get some money it will be useful to pay the loan and for the children's future. He wrote in a paper that after my death give my eyes to my wife.She'll take care of children.He sacrificed his life also.Even after his death he sacrifices his eyes .

Why should he sacrifice everything. Don't he know to leave agriculture and go to another job.Why should he do this all??? This everything is only for us. If he didn't go to field and get yield how would we live...He sacrifices his assets, his family,his food ,his life and everything .Even after this all sacrifices what did he get ...

According to me farmers are the first Sacrificer .
You say me according to you who is your first Sacrificer???

Quotes On Sacrifice

Even if you are poor if you sacrifice something for others you become rich by your heart.

All can sacrifice for their friends and families when you sacrifice even for your enemies your sacrifice becomes selfless and pure.

Everything around us sacrifices itself for human
But I don't know what humans sacrifices for it.

Sacrifice with benefits for you will never be a fulfilled sacrifice.

If your sacrifice benefits others and not you is the exact meaning of sacrifice.

Punam Nikalje

She is Punam Suresh Nikalje belong from nashik city. She is 17 year's old,eduacation like 12 com appear from KVN Naik Clg. Her Birth date is 9/10/2003,at nashik city, some kind of specialities the are. every work are complete..at the time. She has Many hobbies are there but most important is..reading Her SSC educational series from V.N Naik school, Ranenagar,Cidco, Nashik. for higher education that one KVN Naik Clg of art,com& science.

मेरे साथ तुम हो..!!

मुझे मनाने का तुम बहाना ढूंढ के रखा करो...
मैं रुठ जाऊ तो भी तुम मेरा ख्याल रखा करो...

कहा जायेंगे हम तुझे छोढ़ कर
तेरे बिना रात नहीं गुजरती
तो जिंदगी क्या गुजरेगी...

मैं लब हूं पर मेरी बात तुम हो,
और मैं तब हूं जब मेरे साथ तुम हो..!!

Uske Siva

Uske siva kisi aur ko chahna mere bas me nhi
Ye dil uska hai apna hota toh baat aur thi,

इज़हार -ए मोहब्बत

जब से यार का इज़हार -ए मोहब्बत
हमारा नसीब हो गया,
तब से शहर का हर शक्श
हमारा रकीब हो गया।

तुम्हारे ख्वाबों में हमें...
आसरा मिल गया हैं......
तुम्हारे अहसास ने हमें...
मंजिल दिखा दिया हैं....
तुम्हारे इश्क ने हमें
अपना बना लिया है....

हम तो वो है जो तेरी बाते सुनकर तेरे हो गए,

वो और होंगे जिन्हें मोहब्बत चेहरे से होती होगी...

Flairs and Glairs, a platform by a student for the students. We are esteemed youth struggling to carve out our path for our future and we follow a basic mindset Since everyone is not born with aHround skills. Joining hands with people who are born to execute it wit   h perfection is the best way to evolve. Self -Evolution is the need of the hour but, evolving as a community is what we strive for.   The initiative as kickstarted by, Founder - Mr. Shubham Shah with the motive to utilize the skillset and talent of writing has now a team of 10+ people who are actively participating into newer forms of learning and discovering talents among youngsters. We Provide platform and services like Publishing opportunities, Open mics, Workshops, Hands-on training. Operating with Brand Name of Flairs and Glairs (Publication House), we offer the chance of elevating a passionate writer to an esteemed author   With Brand name Teekhe Zasbaaat. We bring to you an opportunity to get accustomed with the Public Speaking and Presenting of Thoughts along with regular challenges to brush up your inking spirit.   The newest initiative to extend our services we introduced in a new writing Platform- The Glittering Fables and Ink Over Tears.

We Choose to Fly Like A Falcon than to be

a Leg Pulling Crab.

To Know More: Infoline – 7781900870
Mail Us At-
flairsandglairs@gmail.com / info@flairsandglairs.in
Or Visit is at
www.flairsandglairs.com / www.flairsandglairs.in
Social Handles- @flairsandglairs @teekhezasbaaat

www.ingramcontent.com/pod-product-compliance
Lightning Source LLC
Chambersburg PA
CBHW070542160726

48003CB00004B/1840